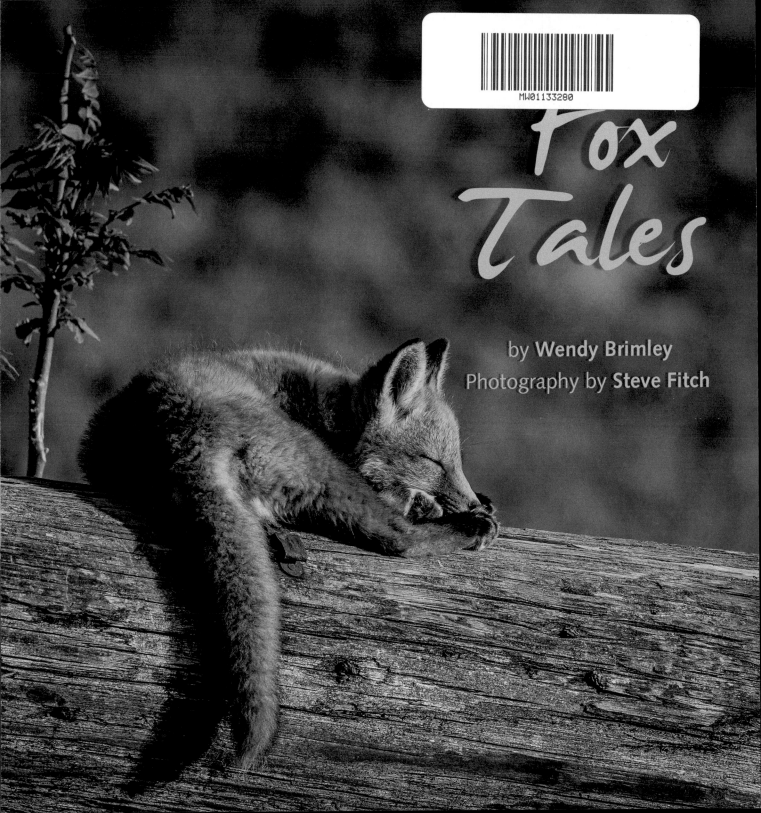

Fox
Tales

by **Wendy Brimley**
Photography by **Steve Fitch**

Fox Tales

iUniverse books may be ordered through booksellers or by contacting:

iUniverse
1663 Liberty Drive
Bloomington, IN 47403
www.iuniverse.com
844-349-9409

Because of the dynamic nature of the Internet, any web addresses or links contained in this book may have changed since publication and may no longer be valid. The views expressed in this work are solely those of the author and do not necessarily reflect the views of the publisher, and the publisher hereby disclaims any responsibility for them.

Any people depicted in stock imagery provided by Getty Images are models, and such images are being used for illustrative purposes only.
Certain stock imagery © Getty Images.

ISBN: 978-1-6632-4589-2 (sc)
ISBN: 978-1-6632-4590-8 (e)

Library of Congress Control Number: 2022917836

Print information available on the last page.

iUniverse rev. date: 09/29/2022

Fox Tales

Steve Fitch

Wendy Brimley

Fiona was a beautiful red fox who lived on the outer edge of a farm. She had huge honey-colored eyes, a black nose, and a shiny red blond coat. Her front legs were black like she wore long socks! Female foxes are also called "vixen". Fiona made her home in a small fox hole called a den. It was near the edge of a forest that overlooked a thick green cow pasture. Fiona liked to chase chipmunks and play in the fields and grasses. She was happy there but she was very lonely.

One day Fiona met Felix, a handsome male fox. Male foxes are called "dog foxes". Felix had a snowy white beard of fur on his neck and chest and intelligent light brown eyes. Felix was just passing by the farm looking for company.

One look at Fiona and Felix was captivated! "Hellooo, beautiful lady!" Felix crooned. Fiona blinked at Felix, then shyly looked away. "Hello…" she said. She looked back and their eyes met. The two foxes instantly fell in love! So, they decided to get married. They asked their neighbor, Reverend Charles Woodchuck, to perform the ceremony.

Reverend Charles, who his friends called Chuck, lived in a deep tunnel he had dug nearby called a burrow. He liked to snack on sweet grasses and relax in the sun.

He took one look at Felix and Fiona and knew they were made for each other. He married them on the spot. The newlywed foxes decided to make their home in the den on the farm and they were very happy.

Every day, Fiona and Felix enjoyed frolicking together in the meadows and chasing butterflies and chipmunks. Soon there were three little baby foxes in the family called kits. Fiona and Felix named their kits Freddy, Faye and Fern. Freddy had grey green eyes while Faye and Fern had warm honey-colored eyes like their mother. All three kits had black tips on their red blond ears, soft reddish downy fur and red and grey bushy tails. The five foxes were a very happy family.

Early each morning, before the sun came up,
Felix went out to find food for his growing family.

6

Foxes have whiskers that help them navigate in the dusk and dark. When Felix brought the food back to the den, Fiona would feed their family.

Felix then rested and kept watch for any danger. Later the kits cuddled up to their mom at the back of the den while she told them bedtime stories.

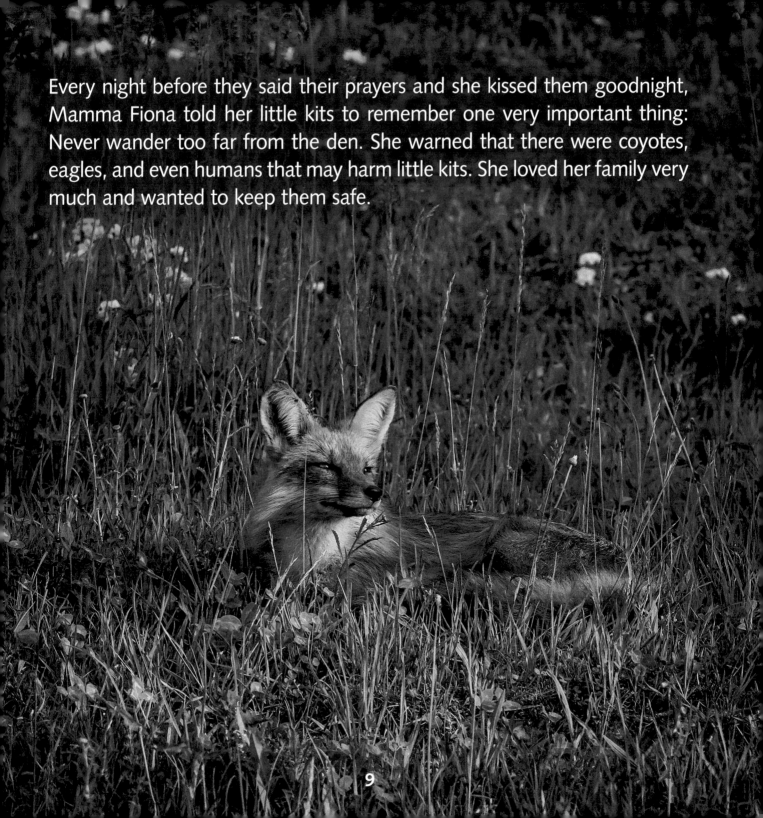

Every night before they said their prayers and she kissed them goodnight, Mamma Fiona told her little kits to remember one very important thing: Never wander too far from the den. She warned that there were coyotes, eagles, and even humans that may harm little kits. She loved her family very much and wanted to keep them safe.

One day when Felix left to look for food, Fiona decided to go along. Their kits were growing fast and the family would need more food to go around. While their parents were away, Freddy, Faye and Fern decided to wander out of the den. The kits loved to romp in the soft green pastures and especially loved to watch the cows and their little calves.

As they wandered, they came upon Reverend Chuck. He was just coming out of his burrow, not being an early riser.

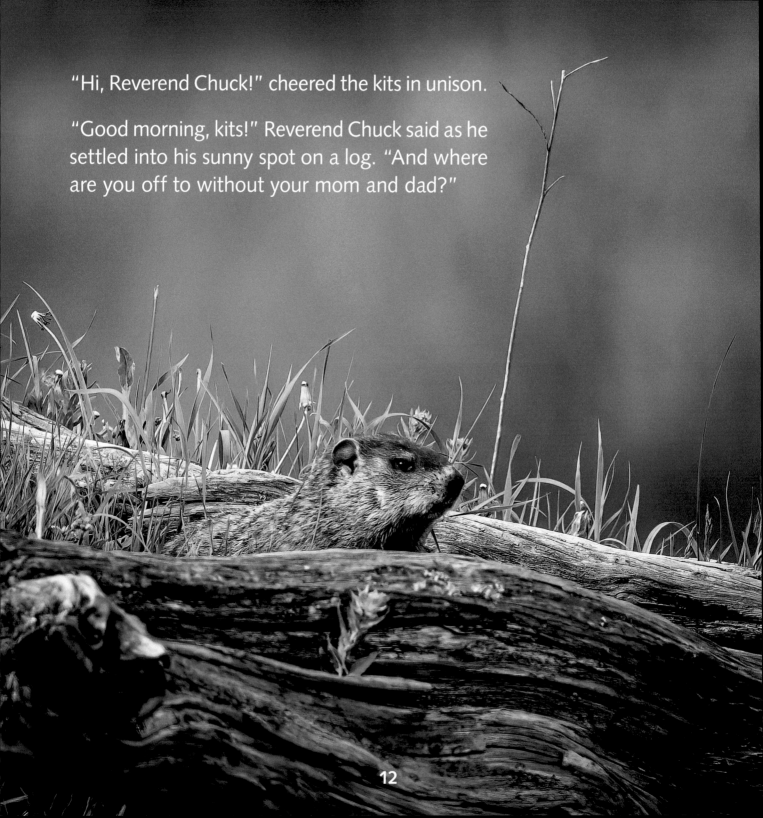

"Hi, Reverend Chuck!" cheered the kits in unison.

"Good morning, kits!" Reverend Chuck said as he settled into his sunny spot on a log. "And where are you off to without your mom and dad?"

"Oh, we're just out playing..." said Freddy casually.

"Ok," said Reverend Chuck, "but don't go too far!" he warned. And with that, he plodded towards the forest to find some sweet grasses for his morning snack.

"We won't" said Freddy as he pranced along, heading deeper into the fields. The kits wandered further away till they were at the fence line to the cow pasture. Freddy nudged Faye and Fern with his shiny black pointed nose. "Let's go play with the calves!" he barked.

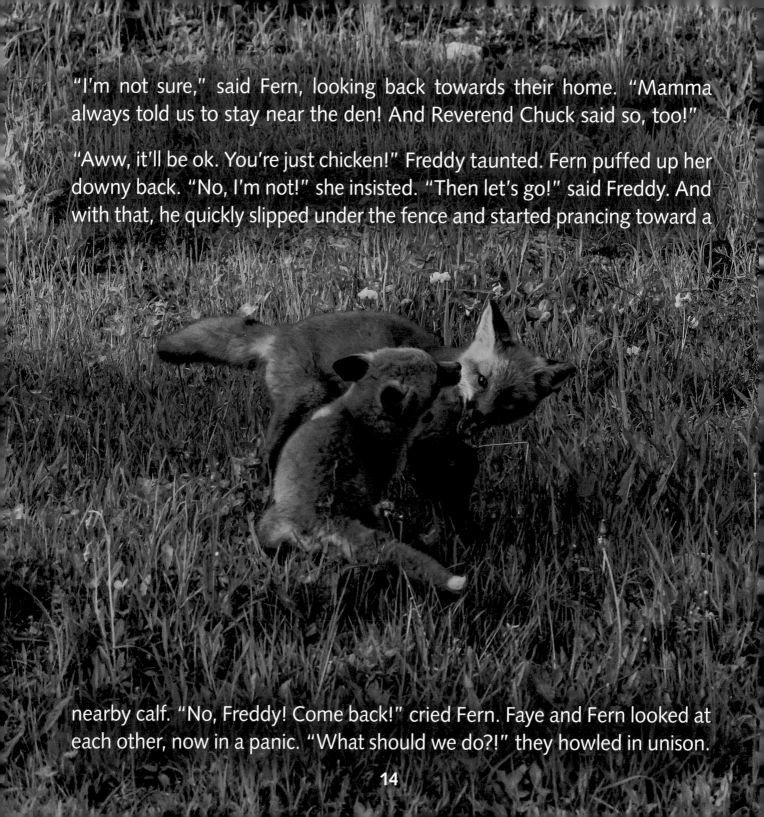

"I'm not sure," said Fern, looking back towards their home. "Mamma always told us to stay near the den! And Reverend Chuck said so, too!"

"Aww, it'll be ok. You're just chicken!" Freddy taunted. Fern puffed up her downy back. "No, I'm not!" she insisted. "Then let's go!" said Freddy. And with that, he quickly slipped under the fence and started prancing toward a

nearby calf. "No, Freddy! Come back!" cried Fern. Faye and Fern looked at each other, now in a panic. "What should we do?!" they howled in unison.

Suddenly, Fern looked up to see a very large bald eagle in the sky.

It was soaring high, slowly passing over the farm. The eagle scanned the ground and spied the downy fur of little Freddy in the wide-open pasture, making his way over to a calf.

"Oh no!" cried Fern. "We have to do something or that big eagle will get Freddy!" Just then Mamma Fiona happened to come by out of the field looking for her kits. She had come home to an empty den and started to worry. "Girls, why are you so far from home?" she asked. "Haven't I warned you about this? And, where's your brother Freddy?"

Fiona followed Fern's gaze over to where Freddy was now a good distance away in the cow pasture. At the same time, she looked up and saw the eagle pumping its wide wings, headed for Freddy. "Faye, Fern, run home to the den!! Now!! Just run!" Faye and Fern were very frightened and they ran as fast as their short furry legs could carry them through the fields towards the den. At the same time, Fiona flattened her slight body and slipped under the fence. She started racing across the pasture towards Freddy. But the eagle with his powerful wings was already fast

approaching the unsuspecting little kit. Thinking fast, Fiona spied some large trees that lined the pasture near the calves. If she could get Freddy scooted safely under the trees, the branches would provide protection.

18

Then the eagle wouldn't be able to reach Freddy and would have to give up the chase. "Freddy!" Fiona howled, long and loud, gaining his attention. "On the double, follow me NOW!"

Freddy was surprised to see Mamma Fiona. He realized he was definitely in deep trouble. But then he saw the eagle circling overhead, coming closer, and knew he was in more danger than just his momma's wrath.

"Coming, Mamma!" Freddy barked, and stretching his legs out as far as he could, he ran towards her.

Fiona sprinted towards the trees with her bushy tail flying. Freddy scampered close behind her. They made it into the soft grasses under the tree branches, gasping for breath. They looked up as the eagle reluctantly turned around and floated back into the sky. Freddy was shaking. "Mamma…" he started, looking tearfully into his momma's eyes.

But Fiona stopped him. "Hush, my son. I'm just so thankful you're safe.

Let's make our way back to the den and check on the girls". Fiona and Freddy picked their way carefully through the fields, making sure there was no further danger. They were greeted at the entrance to the den by Faye and Fern, leaping joyfully at their return.

Fiona noticed Felix's worried look and drew him away. Placing her paw on his downy chest, Fiona whispered, "I think he's learned his lesson. Let's enjoy our family and the food you brought home today. We have a lot to be thankful for." Felix licked the top of Fiona's head and gave her a slow smile. Then he wrapped his paws around her and his kits. The Fox family

celebrated the safe return of their little family and enjoyed their time together in their den on the farm.

The end